Spot's First Christmas

Eric Hill

PUFFIN BOOKS

It's Christmas Eve, Spot...

Wrap the presents neatly, Spot.

Who's outside?

It's time for bed, Spot.

Spot! Go to bed!

Spot is
asleep
at last!

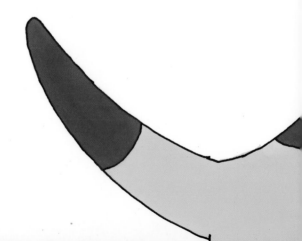

Very early the next morning . . .

A ball, a bone,

a brush. And guess what else?

What a pretty blue collar, Spot.

It's from Santa!

PUFFIN BOOKS

Published by the Penguin Group: London, New York,
Australia, Canada, India, New Zealand and South Africa
Penguin Books Ltd, Registered Offices:
80 Strand, London WC2R 0RL, England

puffinbooks.com

First published by William Heinemann Ltd, 1983
Published in the United States of America by G.P. Putnam's Sons, 1983
Published in Puffin Books, 1986
This colorized edition published by Puffin Books,
a division of Penguin Young Readers Group, 2004

002

Printed and bound in China

ISBN 978-0-14240-202-3